JOURNEY THROUGH the PILLOW CAVE

by Barnaby Stew

bebins books

bebinsbooks.com

ISBN 978-1-950956-40-1 (paperback)

In my room there are toys and things...
funny books and magic rings.

But one small thing that's the best of all
is a stack of pillows by the wall.

"Why," you might ask, "is this thing great?"
Because! Look closely - it's a secret gate!

My name is Annabel, and this is Clyde.
Prepare yourself for a magic ride!
If you have imagination and you're also brave,
adventure awaits in the pillow cave!

With a light to show the way,
we begin exploring.

Deep underground, where cave bats are snoring.

Take a look, way up high.

Glowworms shine like a starlit sky!

Entering the rainforest, we feel quite small

overlooking a thundering waterfall.

See the animals! See the trees!

We swing through the air just like monkeys!

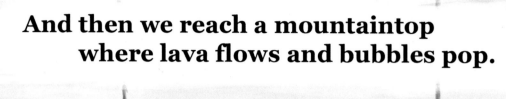

**And then we reach a mountaintop
where lava flows and bubbles pop.**

It's a volcano! We must escape the heat
before the rocks burn up our feet!

We dive into the ocean and swim with pleasure
among sea stars, fish, and sunken treasure.

The clam and the octopus dance in turn.

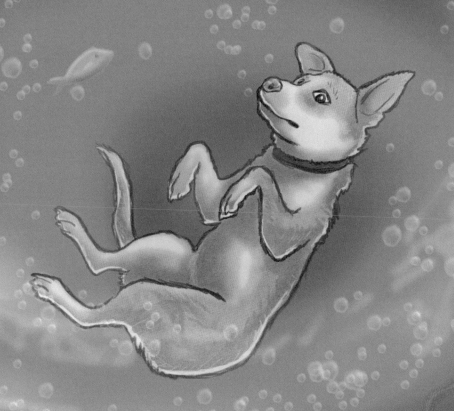

The water is starting to churn...

It looks like our pillows have all fallen down!
But oh, don't you worry - no need to frown.

**Pretending is fun, and easy to do.
We'll make a new cave...**

and so can you!

For more work by Barnaby Stew, visit
barnabystew.com/news